Lulu's House, Wagtail Town, The World, The Universe

Me

Bonnie

She's the smallest

Pom ↘

She's so chirpy

Alfie ↑ My very best friend

Otto ↘

He's very clever

Dear Reader,
This is the second book about Wagtail Town – the best place in the universe. It is the story of what happened when I was looking after Bonnie on the Treasure Hunt and things went a bit wrong...
Lots of love
Lulu
x o x o x
P.S. I was sorry!

↳ Yumi

She's always dreaming

Harvey
→

He's good at acrobatics

the Little Dog with BIG ideas!

AIL END

THE STICKS

BONES MUSEUM

SEEK AND FIND

LIBRARY

NOSE TO TAIL SURGERY

CHEWSY'S

Pete-a-Boudoir

Shampoodles

SWEETNESS & BITE

POM'S HOUSE

HARRY'S HOUSE

BONEO DRIVE

LULU'S HOUSE

POOCH PATROL

DOGGER BANK

First published in paperback in Great Britain by
HarperCollins Publishers Ltd in 2013

1 3 5 7 9 10 8 6 4 2

ISBN: 978-0-00-742517-4

HarperCollins Children's Books is a division of HarperCollins Publishers Ltd.

Text and illustrations copyright © Emma Chichester Clark 2013

Visit our website at: www.harpercollins.co.uk

Printed in China

Hurry up, Harvey!

Wagtail Town Lulu and the Treasure Hunt!

Emma Chichester Clark

HarperCollins *Children's Books*

Over the hills and far away there's a lovely place called Wagtail Town where Lulu lives. One day, when Lulu went to school, Miss Ellie said,
"Today we're going to have a **treasure hunt!**"

"Oooh la la!" cried Lulu. "I **love** treasure!"

"How do we find it?" asked Otto.

"We have to look for clues," said Alfie.

"Then we follow them," said Pom.

"And then we'll find treasure!" said Yumi.

"I'll find it first!" said Harvey.

Miss Ellie told everyone there were six clues. The first was a picture of a swing. "Can you guess where it's telling you to go?" she asked.

"I know! I know!" cried Lulu. "It's the park! Come on, Alfie!" Alfie was her very best friend.

Bonnie didn't say anything.

"Before you all go," said Miss Ellie, "I'd like someone to look after Bonnie because she is the smallest."

"I will!" cried Lulu.

"That's very kind of you, Lulu," said Miss Ellie. "Please can you make sure Bonnie doesn't get left behind?"

Lulu took Bonnie's paw. "I'll take care of you Bonnie," she said.

They all went into the park where Mr Mabinty, the park keeper, was waiting for them. "Now, don't forget, you must stay in the park and I'm here if you need me," he said.

"Come on, Bonnie!" cried Lulu. "We're going to find the clue first! Let's go, go, **go!**"

Where are they going?

It's a treasure hunt!

And Lulu's looking after Bonnie!

Bonnie couldn't run as fast as all the others because she was the smallest, so when Lulu and Bonnie caught up, Harvey had already found the second clue. "Here it is!" he said proudly.

"It's the slide!" said Pom. "Come on, everyone!"

And they all rushed off.

Bonnie was going as fast as she could, but she was very slow and Lulu could see that the others were almost at the slide.

"Come on, Bonnie!" she said, gently pulling her along. "Let's go, go, go! A little bit faster if you can!"

Come on, Lulu and Bonnie!

But Bonnie *was* going as fast as she could.

Otto found the third clue at the top of the slide.
It was a picture of a trumpet.

"Rooty-toot-toot!"
chirped Pom.

"It must mean the bandstand!" cried Yumi.
"Come on, everyone!"

They all slid down.

All except Bonnie.
"I *can't*!" she said.

"Yes, you *can*!" said Lulu.
"Come on! I'll catch you!"

Bonnie shut her eyes
and slid down the slide.

Lulu helped her up.
"Now let's **go!**" she cried.
"As fast as you can!"

The others were nearly
at the bandstand.

"Oh, Bonnie, *please*, can't you go any faster?" said Lulu. "I **really**, **really** want to find a clue!"

Over at the bandstand, Lulu could see Pom had already found the next one. "Here it is!" she cried.

"Oh, no!"

"Look! It's a birds' nest," said Yumi.

"Birds' nests are in trees!" said Otto.

"But which one?" asked Harvey. "There are millions!"

"Let's go and see!" said Alfie. "Come on, Lulu!"

"But Bonnie's **so slow!**" cried Lulu. "Oh, hurry up, Bonnie!"

There were lots of different kinds of trees.
Lulu could see the others searching, high and low.

"It's not here!"
said Yumi.

"And it's not
here!" said Otto.

"It's not anywhere
in this one!" said Pom.

"And it's not in this
one either," said Harvey.

"Here it is!" cried Alfie. He held up a picture of the fountain.

"Oh, bother! Now there's only one more clue!" said Lulu. "Come on, Bonnie! Let's go, go, go!"

"Wait!" wailed Bonnie. **"I'm stuck!"**

And she turned...

But Lulu just couldn't
wait any longer.

...and ran to catch
up with the others.

She'd had an idea...
"Wait there, Bonnie!
I promise I'll come back,"
she cried.

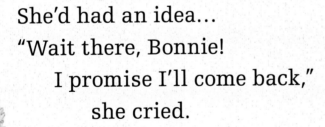

Everyone stopped.

"Where's Bonnie?" asked Alfie.

"Wait for me!"
cried Lulu.

"**Um...**" said Lulu.
She looked around.
"Well..."

"But Lulu, you were supposed to look after Bonnie and make sure she wasn't left behind," said Alfie.

"She's not exactly left behind..." said Lulu. "She's just waiting... in a tree..."

They all stared at Lulu.

"...it's just that I wanted to find the last clue..." she said.

Lulu's eyes filled with tears.
She knew she'd done a terrible thing.

"We'd better go and find Bonnie,"
said Alfie. "Lulu, you stay here."

And they all walked away and left
Lulu on her own.

Lulu sat alone by the
fountain. A tear trickled
down her nose. Now she
knew what it felt like
to be left behind.

"It wasn't Bonnie's fault she was so slow..." thought Lulu. "A *real* friend would have waited. I promised to look after her and I didn't do a very good job."

Just then, Mr Mabinty appeared pushing his wheelbarrow. "Hallo, Lulu," he said. "You look a bit glum. What's the matter?"

"Oh, **everything**," said Lulu sadly. "I wish I could start today all over again!"

"Oh dear!" said Mr Mabinty. "Well, I've found something that might cheer you up!"

"Surprise!"
Bonnie jumped out of the
wheelbarrow!

"Bonnie!" said Lulu. "I'm so
sorry I left you behind."

"It's all right," said Bonnie. "I
know you didn't really mean to."

"I promise I'll **never, ever**
do it again," said Lulu.

Then Bonnie giggled.

"What's so funny?"
asked Lulu.

"I think you might have found the last clue after all!" said Bonnie.

And there it was! Stuck on Lulu's bottom! She'd been sitting on it all the time.

"Oooh la la!" cried Lulu. "The last clue is the trampoline!"

When the others came back, they were very pleased to see Bonnie. She showed them the final clue.

"Come on, let's go, go, go!" cried Bonnie.

"But this time let's stick together," said Lulu, taking Bonnie's paw. "It's much more fun that way."

And because she was the smallest, Bonnie saw the treasure first.

It was under the table beside the trampoline in a *real* treasure chest.

"Let's open it!" cried Otto.

"I think Bonnie should open it," said Lulu.

So Bonnie did.
"Chocolate bones!" she cried.

There was one for everyone.

"If it hadn't been for Bonnie being so small, we would never have found the last clue *or* the treasure!" said Lulu.

"Where was the last clue?" asked Alfie.

Bonnie and Lulu giggled. "It was stuck to Lulu's bottom!" said Bonnie, and everyone laughed and laughed and laughed.

And after they'd finished their chocolate bones, they all had
a bounce on the trampoline, up and down, high in the air.

So, at the end of another busy day...

The moon came up,
The sun went down,
And all was well
In Wagtail Town.

For the volunteers and staff of Home-Start and to the families
with young children who they support across the UK.
www.home-start.org.uk
P.G.

For my brother, Charlie.
S.U.

MIX
Paper from
responsible sources
FSC® C012700

EGMONT

We bring stories to life

First published in Great Britain 2016
by Egmont UK Limited
The Yellow Building, 1 Nicholas Road, London W11 4AN
www.egmont.co.uk

Text copyright © Pippa Goodhart 2016
Illustrations copyright © Sam Usher 2016

The author and illustrator have asserted their moral rights.

ISBN 978 1 4052 7510 1

A CIP catalogue record for this title is available from the
British Library.

WHAT WILL DANNY DO TODAY?

Pippa Goodhart & Sam Usher

EGMONT

What will Danny wear today?

Will he choose spotty, stripy or plain clothes?

Will he pick a crunchy,
chewy or wobbly breakfast?

What do you think he'll drink?

After Danny has waved goodbye to his dad,
will he pedal or zip, walk, ride or skip to school?

SCHOOL

What lessons will Danny have?

Rocket building? Painting?
Or playing the piano?

Who will teach Danny today?
Who do you think his
favourite teacher is?

LOST MUG

When it's time for PE, will Danny run, jump or hit balls?

Will he slide, swing or see-saw at playtime?

In the afternoon, everyone is cutting or sticking or painting.

What will
Danny make?

Danny's dad is collecting him after school. He's wearing a green jacket – can you spot him?

Will Danny skate, row or
watch a film for his special
treat after school?

After his busy day,
which book will
Danny take to bed?

Look! He's chosen the one that you've just read!